MICHELANGELO

Michelangelo, the youngest and most energetic of the Turtles, is also the friendliest and most lighthearted. He'd rather solve a problem with a joke than a fight.

NUNCHUCKS

Michelangelo's weapons of choice are *nunchucks*. Made of two hard sticks connected by a chain, *nunchucks* can be spun to deliver a striking blow, or they can be used defensively.

NINJAS IN TRAINING!

"WHO NEEDED
MATURITY
WHEN WE HAD OUR
MAD NINJA CHOPS?"

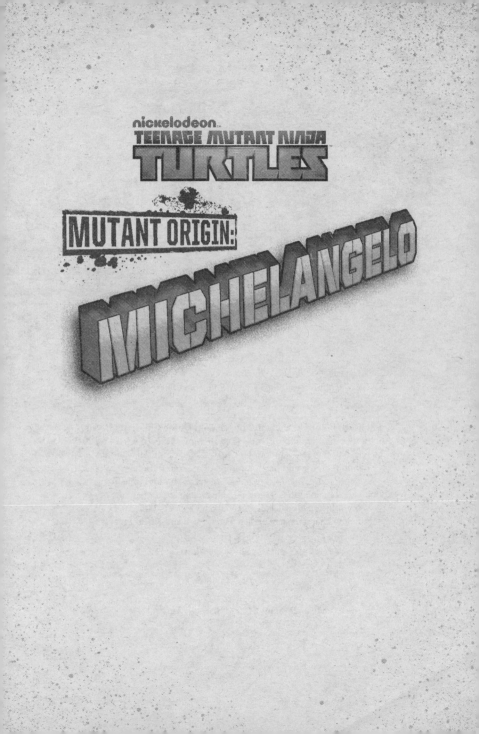

Published in the United States by Random House Children's Books,
a division of Random House, Inc., 1745 Broadway, New York, NY 10019,
and in Canada by Random House of Canada Limited, Toronto.
Random House and the colophon are registered trademarks of
Random House, Inc. Nickelodeon, Teenage Mutant Ninja Turtles,
and all related titles, logos, and characters are trademarks of
Viacom International Inc. and Viacom Overseas Holdings C.V.
Based on characters created by Peter Laird and Kevin Eastman.

randomhouse.com/kids

ISBN: 978-0-449-80994-5

Printed in the United States of America
10 9

nickelodeon
TEENAGE MUTANT NINJA
TURTLES

MUTANT ORIGIN:

MICHELANGELO

Adapted by Michael Teitelbaum

Based on the teleplay "Day One, Part One"
by Joshua Sternin and Jeffrey Ventimilia

RANDOM HOUSE 🏠 NEW YORK

CHAPTER 1

I am a turtle.

I know, I know. Turtles can't talk. Turtles are small, round animals that live in plastic aquariums, sitting under little plastic palm trees and not moving very much.

Well, believe it or not, that's how my life began.

My name's Michelangelo, by the way,

and this is the story of
how my three brothers—Raphael,
Leonardo, and Donatello—and I all went
from being those tiny creatures humans
love to keep as pets to becoming lean,
mean, well-oiled fighting machines of ninja
stealth, power, and smarts.

Master Splinter—he's our ninja
teacher, our sensei, and as much of a
father as we've ever known—stood in the
training room, just watching us. I always
know he's going to say something important when he's silent like that.

"Michelangelo, you will now spar with
Leonardo," Splinter said. "Begin."

Get psyched! I've always liked sparring with my brother Leonardo. He's the

most skilled of us all in ninja combat and defensive techniques, and man, do I learn a lot fighting him. Sometimes I can even beat him.

I stepped over to Leonardo. We both bowed and gripped our weapons tightly—Leonardo had grabbed his double swords, and I, well, I had my trusty *nunchucks*.

Then it began.

My brother is a really good fighter, so I need to be quick and clever to beat him. I ducked, spun, and rolled on the floor, popping up into an attack pose.

Oh, he's good, my brother Leo. His defensive postures mimicked my every move. So I figured maybe a little trash talk would throw him off guard. That, *I'm* really good at!

"Oh, yeah," I said, spinning my *nun-*

chucks right in front of Leonardo's face. "Michelangelo is on the move! You don't know what to do! You have no clue how to stop me."

I spun into a forward roll, ending up behind Leonardo. Mikey, the stealth ninja!

"I'm here!" I announced, whipping into a backflip. "I'm there!" I spun my *nunchucks* again. "I could be anywhere. I ask you . . . how do you stop what you can't even see?"

Yeah, I had him right where I wanted him.

He was confused. He'd lowered his weapon and was just staring at me as if I were no threat to him at all. I was ready to take him down!

I launched my sleek, athletic body into

another forward roll. I was going to come up and out of this roll right in Leo's—

Omph!

Leonardo caught me square in the midsection with the butt of his sword, as if he had been timing my moves right from the start. Which, come to think of it, he probably had.

The air shot out of my lungs. I was doubled over, waving my hands, unable to speak. Mikey, the stealth ninja, needed to lie down!

"*That's* how I stop what I can't even see, to answer your question," Leonardo said calmly. "And by the way—I *can* see you, Mikey."

My breath slowly started to return. "Good one, Leo," I wheezed, collapsing onto the floor. "I'll just sit right here and watch Raph and Donnie for a while."

Leonardo stepped to the side of the training room and stood next to Master Splinter.

I looked up from the floor to see Donatello and Raphael circling each other, sizing each other up. Donatello spun his six-foot staff in a circle, switching it

smoothly from hand to hand. Raphael twirled his *sais,* two thin daggers with wicked-sharp points.

We'd been training like this against each other for years. After all, who else could we train against? Master Splinter didn't allow us to leave our underground lair. We knew each other's strengths and weaknesses pretty well. But part of being a great ninja is always being full of surprises. That, and having a really hard shell.

"All right, Donnie, put down the staff and no one gets hurt," Raphael said, his eyes locked firmly on Donatello's. Donnie smiled. "You said that last time, Raph," he pointed out. "And then you went ahead and hurt me."

Now it was Raph's turn to smile. "Yeah, but less than I would have," he explained.

"Yeah, right," Donatello replied, not believing a word of it.

Raphael's *my* brother, too, and I didn't buy it, either.

Donatello attacked using lightning-fast moves, flashing both ends of his staff, striking high and low. He drove Raphael back, directing blows at his head, his ankles, his midsection, and his legs.

But Raphael was just as fast and totally calm—well, calm for him, anyway. Raph has a pretty harsh temper, and sometimes he lets it get the better of him when he's fighting.

Not that day. He blocked each of Donatello's blows, redirecting the staff with his *sai* blades. Donnie lunged at Raphael, but Raph sidestepped the attack and snatched Donnie's staff, his hands moving faster than a lizard's tongue . . . or maybe a turtle's tongue. Nah, lizards' tongues move faster. I think.

Raphael holstered his *sais,* snapped the staff in two over his knee, then began hitting Donatello with the two pieces, one in each hand.

Donnie dropped to the floor and pulled his limbs into his shell for protection.

"Okay! Okay! I'm down!" Donnie shouted as Raph kept whacking him.

Raph tossed away the broken staff. Donnie peeked out of his shell to see if the attack was over yet. Having just kicked one brother's butt, Raphael turned his sights on another. Luckily, it wasn't me!

Raphael drew his *sais* and turned to face Leonardo, who pulled out his own double swords and bowed. Raph bowed back, but impatiently. Raphael has never been one for the fine points of ninja combat rituals, the little things Master Splinter always tells us are important for focus, respect, and honor. Or is it honor, respect, and focus?

Raph is more about kickin' butt than about honor and all that, but Leonardo, well, he follows the rules. He's a by-the-book kinda turtle.

"*Onegai shimasu!*" Leonardo shouted. That's the formal challenge to combat.

"Whatever you say," Raphael replied.

What came next was an awesome display of speed and skill. Because Raph and Leo have battled so many times, they knew each other's every move. Watching my brothers, I wondered if I would ever be good enough to beat either of them. But mostly it made me glad that if we ever got the chance to battle real bad guys, these two dudes would be on *my* side.

Raphael's style is totally wild. He's like a windmill with swords. Like a propeller blade with sharp stuff at the end. He never stops moving. Just when you think he's about to come after you . . . he's already there.

But Leonardo is really good. I mean, ultra really good. He's got all that technical fighting stuff down. So even though Raph comes at him like a buzz saw, Leo can handle the attack. Did I say that he's really good? Thought so.

Raphael attacked like a madman. Now, I know my brother Leo, and all that madman stuff is not for him. He sticks to the rules. He does what he's been taught to do. Spinning and swinging, Raph broke through Leo's defense and knocked the double swords from Leo's hands. Raph grabbed him and slammed his butt to the mat.

Score one for the madman!

Leonardo landed hard, but I think he was more embarrassed than hurt.

"*Ya me!*" Master Splinter shouted. That meant it was the end of the practice session.

Leo rolled up to his feet and brushed himself off.

"You all did very well," Master Splinter announced.

"But I did better than the others," Raphael boasted.

"This training exercise is about self-improvement for each of you," Master Splinter explained. "It is not about winning and losing."

Raphael lowered his head. For a second I actually thought he was being humble. Yeah, right. "Raphael" and "humble" . . . You are *not* going to hear those two words in the same sentence!

"I know, Sensei," Raph said softly. Then he quickly added, "But I won. And they lost."

Master Splinter didn't say a word. He

just stuck out one finger and pressed it against the side of Raphael's head.

Raph lifted himself up onto his toes. I could tell by how his face was all scrunched up that it really, really hurt.

"Ah! Ah! Ah!" Raphael cried. "But what's really important, of course, is that we all did our best! Good job, everyone!"

Master Splinter smiled and let him go.

Sometimes it takes a little extra convincing for Raph to get the point. Master Splinter is good at that!

CHAPTER 2

The best part of sparring is that it really works up an appetite, so when I finally get to sit down and eat, everything tastes that much better. And I love eating. In fact, the only thing I like more than eating is . . . is . . . uh, I'll have to get back to you on that one!

My brothers and I hunkered down around the kitchen table with Master

Splinter. We dug into a scrumptious dinner of algae and worms. Yum, yum! Last night's dinner was worms and algae, so this was a nice change.

I shoveled another forkful into my mouth, then looked around. My brothers were all slumped down in their seats, patting their stomachs.

"There's a little more algae and worms left if anybody wants it," I announced. "Anybody? Anybody? Raph?"

"That's okay, I'm good," Raph said, waving me off.

Hmm . . . Raph had only had three portions. Maybe he wasn't feeling well.

"No thanks," Donnie said.

"All yours, Mikey," Leo added.

I stood up. It was time to reveal the surprise I had planned for everyone.

"Well then," I said. "I guess no one left room for . . ."

I did three backflips over to the fridge, opened the door, and pulled out a . . .

"Cake!" I announced, setting it down on the table.

"It *is* a cake!" Donnie said.

I couldn't wait for him to taste it.

Raphael leaned in close to the cake.

"And it's made of algae and worms."

"Yup," I said. "Only the best for my bros."

"What's the icing made of?" Leonardo asked.

"You don't want to know," I said. "Come on, guys, aren't you even curious about why I made a cake?"

I couldn't wait any longer. I guess no one else had figured it out.

"Happy Mutation Day!" I shouted.

"Happy Mutation Day!" my three brothers shouted back.

Master Splinter smiled, but he looked kind of sad. I could almost see his mind racing back to that amazing day. "Ah, yes. Mutation Day. Fifteen years ago today our lives changed forever and we became the unlikeliest of families."

This is the part I like best.

"Tell us the story, Master Splinter!" I said, pulling my chair in close so I wouldn't miss a single word.

"Michelangelo, I have already told it many times," Master Splinter reminded me.

"Please? *Pleeeeeeeaaase?*"

Raphael put his hand over my mouth.

"Please, Sensei?" Raph said. "It's the only way to shut Mikey up."

"Very well," said Master Splinter. He took a deep breath, then began. "Fifteen years ago, when I was still human, I was leaving a pet store carrying a glass bowl containing four baby turtles I had just picked up as pets."

"Ooh, ooh, that was us!" I cried.

"Yes, Michelangelo. And don't interrupt." Master Splinter continued. "The pet store was having a sale. Four turtles for a dollar, including the marbles and the little plastic palm tree.

"On my way home, I passed a strange man on the street. Something felt 'off' about him. Something was wrong, but I couldn't quite put my finger on it. I decided to follow him, and ended up tracking him into an alley. It was a filthy place. Garbage swirled in gusts of wind. I felt a rat scurry up my leg."

"Ewww!" I said. "I'm glad that didn't happen to me."

"Hey, Mikey, he told you to stop interrupting," Raphael chided me.

"Stopping now," I said. Sometimes I get a little overexcited.

Master Splinter continued.

"As I shook the rat off my leg, I noticed that the strange man I had followed was

being given an odd-looking canister by another man, who I could not see clearly, as he was hidden in the shadows. I tried to keep myself out of view, but two other men stepped up behind me."

"'Go no further!' one of the men shouted. 'This place is a place where you are not allowed to be in this place.'"

That dude talked so weird. It still creeps me out when I think about it.

"'I was just leaving,' I said to the men," Master Splinter went on. "I was hoping to slip out of the alley and avoid what would probably become an unpleasant confrontation. I was, after all, greatly outnumbered.

"'We have been seen in this place by you, so this is not a place that will be left by you,' a second man said to me."

"Why did they talk so strange?" Donatello asked.

He got to ask exactly what I was thinking! Now I figured Master Splinter would tell *him* not to interrupt.

"I did not have time to ask," Master Splinter told Donnie.

I guess I'm the only one who can't interrupt!

"I quickly realized that I would not leave that alley without a fight. I placed the bowl containing you four off to the side, composed myself, and began a series of ninja self-defense techniques—many of the same techniques I have attempted to teach you.

"I was surprised and pleased to discover that these strange men who talked funny moved awkwardly. They posed little challenge to a trained ninja, and I subdued them quite easily.

"However, just before he ran off, the man who had been carrying the strange-looking canister threw it at me. I managed to duck out of the way, but the canister smashed into the wall. It split open and a thick, glowing green ooze poured out, splashing all over my body.

"I screamed in pain, noticing that the rat I had flung off my leg earlier had returned to my ankle and was also covered in the green ooze. I stumbled backward and knocked over the bowl containing you four.

"You all spilled out of the bowl and landed in a puddle of the green ooze. We all began to mutate instantly. I transformed into a giant rat with my human brain and

ninja skills intact. And of course, you four transformed into the humanoid turtles you are today."

I wiped a tear from the corner of my eye. No matter how many times I hear that story, it always chokes me up.

"That was the beginning of our life together," Master Splinter said, reaching up to a shelf and taking down a smashed-up canister. "It was the mysterious substance in this canister that, in a way, gave birth to us all."

It was like meeting my parent for the first time. Like I had been an orphan all my life until then. I almost cried with happiness. I took the canister from Master Splinter's hand and hugged it.

"Mom!" I cried.

Raphael looked at me and shook his head.

"What?" I asked as a tear rolled down my face. "Can't a guy cry when he's hugging his mom?"

"So, Sensei," Leonardo began, speaking slowly and evenly. "Now that we're fifteen, I think we're ready to finally go up to the surface, don't you?"

I knew what was coming next, so I braced myself for a great big NO!

"Yes . . . ," Master Splinter replied.

Wow! He'd said yes. I had NOT seen that coming at all. I couldn't believe it. We were going up to the surface! We were gonna explore the city, get out into the world, and fight bad guys while cool music played in the background. Or did that only happen on TV?

"Thank you," Donnie said.

"Very cool," Raph added.

". . . and no," Sensei completed his answer.

Oh, man. There was that word. I really don't like "no." It means, well, NO!

"I hate when he does that 'yes . . . and no' thing," Raphael groaned.

"You four have grown powerful," Master Splinter continued. "But you are still young. You lack the maturity to use your skills wisely."

Who needed maturity when we had our mad ninja chops? I wanted to shout, "Just turn us loose, Sensei, and we will own that town up there, wherever that is."

Donnie scratched his head in confusion. "So, Sensei, isn't that just no?"

"Yes . . . ," Master Splinter replied.

Then why didn't he just say no instead of putting us through this whole thing?

". . . and no."

He did it again!

"Wisdom comes from experience, and experience comes from making mistakes."

Donnie leaned forward. "Aha! So in order for us to gain the wisdom, we have to make the mistakes. So that means we *can* go!"

"No."

". . . and yes?" Donnie asked hopefully.

"No."

Donatello slumped back into his chair and sighed in frustration. Master Splinter turned and started to walk away. In *his* mind the conversation was over.

I thought about what Master Splinter had said. If we needed to have wisdom before he'd let us go up to the surface, and we needed to have experience to gain wisdom, but he wasn't letting us go up to the surface to get that experience, how would we ever get wisdom?

All that thinking just made me more confused. Master Splinter had said that experience comes from making mistakes. I don't like to call what I do sometimes "mistakes." I prefer to call it "making it up as I go along."

Leonardo spoke up. "Sensei, we know that you're trying to protect us, but we can't spend our whole lives hiding down here."

Leave it to Leo to put it perfectly . . . I think.

Master Splinter stopped and turned back to face us. We all looked up, waiting for what he was going to say next. He looked at each of us, his eyes moving from face to face.

"You speak wisely, Leonardo," he finally said with a big sigh. "I cannot hold you back forever. You may go. Tonight."

I was waiting for the ". . . and no" part.

But it never came! He must have really meant it this time.

"Yay!" I shouted, lifting my right hand into the air. "High-three!"

"High-three!" my brothers all shouted, and we slapped our hands together over our heads.

I love doing that!

We were going up to the surface. That night! I couldn't believe it!

CHAPTER 3

I peeked into the large common area we use as our main hangout when we're not training. As usual, Leonardo was watching his favorite TV show, *Space Heroes,* a program about the adventures of the crew of a spaceship. I don't really get it. I think it's kinda lame, actually, but Leo lives for it, and he knows every word by heart. It's hard to believe that a smart, serious guy like Leo really enjoys a show like this.

"I have a bold and daring plan," Captain Ryan's voice blared from the TV. "There's no time for hesitation. My orders must be carried out without question!"

Leonardo mouthed every word along with his hero, Captain Ryan.

"Aye, sir!" the whole crew of the space cruiser *Dauntless* shouted together.

At that point, Raphael leaned over Leo's shoulder and said, "You know this is stupid, right?" He's not exactly shy with his opinions.

"*Space Heroes* is a great show," Leo snapped back. "And Captain Ryan is a great hero. Someday I'm going to be just like him."

I tried to picture Leonardo as our leader, barking out orders for my brothers and me to follow without question. Yeah, right, like that would happen.

"Well, you do like to hear yourself talk," Raphael said. "So you're well on your way to being just like him."

Donatello tapped me on the shoulder.

"It's time," he said. "Let's go."

Donnie and I ran into the common room. "It's go time, boys!" I shouted.

I could hardly believe we were heading up to the world of humans, leaving the safety—and boredom—of our underground lair to explore the big bad city. Oh, yeah, I was one psyched Turtle!

Each of us put on our weapon. I always loved this part. Usually it was just to train. But today . . . oh, yeah, today was going to be the real thing. We were four plugged-in Turtles!

When we were ready, Master Splinter gave us a little pep talk.

"You are going up to a strange and hostile world," he began.

Maybe I was wrong—it wouldn't be the first time—but I thought I heard a little bit of sadness in his voice.

He continued. "You must maintain awareness at all times."

"*Hai,* Sensei!" we all shouted. That's the traditional ninja manner of showing respect.

We all turned and headed for the exit, but Sensei wasn't done.

"Remember, stay in the shadows!" Master Splinter added.

We stopped suddenly, crashing into each other. I bumped my head into the back of Donnie's shell.

"*Hai,* Sensei!"

We scrambled toward the exit.

"Wait!" Sensei shouted.

We stopped again.

"Don't talk to strangers."

"*Hai,* Sensei!"

"And everyone is a stranger!"

Okay, this was getting a little annoying. I wanted to get out of there and up to the surface before Master Splinter changed his mind! Or before we turned sixteen.

"*Hai,* Sensei," we all said, this time with way less enthusiasm.

"And everyone make sure you go before you leave," Sensei went on. "The restrooms up there are filthy!"

"Sensei!" we shouted impatiently.

Master Splinter sighed. "Good luck, my sons," he said softly.

We looked at each other, then back at Sensei. He stayed quiet for a couple of seconds, so we bolted for the exit before he could say anything else.

"Here we go!" Donatello shouted.

"This is gonna be so epic!" I said.

"I am so pumped!" Raphael yelled.

"Surface time, boys. Let's do it!" Leonardo added.

As I reached the top of the ladder leading out of our lair, I heard Master Splinter shout up to us: "And look both ways before crossing the street!"

CHAPTER 4

We reached the top of the ladder leading out of our lair.

"Ready, boys?" Leonardo asked.

"Do it, Leo," Raphael said.

Leonardo slowly pushed up on the round metal disc that sits in the hole at the top of our lair. I think Master Splinter calls it a "manhole cover," though I have no idea why a man would dig a hole and then cover it.

When the cover was completely off, Leo stuck his head out.

"Oh, wow!" he said.

"What? What?" Raph asked impatiently.

"Oh, my!" Leo added.

"'Oh, wow! Oh, my!' What are you seeing, Leo?" Raph asked.

"Oh, boy!"

"That's it!" Raph shouted. "Outta my way!"

Raphael climbed over Leonardo and scrambled out of the hole into the world above. Leo climbed out next, and then Donnie.

Then it was my turn.

I stuck my head out of the manhole and immediately understood why Leonardo was so amazed. The night was lit by bright, flashing signs. It was just like TV except with more garbage and a guy sleeping under a newspaper. I could hear a siren way off in the distance.

My heart caught in my throat. I was finally out, finally up in the world of humans.

"It's all so beautiful!" I cried.

That was when I heard a deep rumbling. Then I heard my brothers all yelling at me.

"Get out of the street!"

"Mikey, move!"

"There's a big truck coming!"

A big what? I wondered.

Just as I turned around, I spotted two bright lights barreling toward me.

"Yaaaa!" I shouted. I felt two powerful hands grip my shoulders and yank me up and out of the manhole.

Raphael dragged me to the sidewalk just as a huge truck rolled past the spot where my head had been a moment before.

"I know you don't use your head all that much, Mikey," Raph said. "But I thought you might want to keep it attached to your body for a little while longer."

"Good point, Raph," I said. "Thanks."

"Come on," Leonardo said. "Let's explore."

"Coming!" I shouted, and followed my brothers down the sidewalk.

THE STORY DOESN'T END
HERE! FLIP YOUR BOOK
OVER AND LET RAPHAEL
TELL YOU THE REST OF
THE ADVENTURE!

RAPHAEL

Raphael is the biggest and toughest of the Turtles. He doesn't have time for stealth—he'd rather meet a foe head-on. Raphael might question his brothers' plans and tactics, but he's always ready to fight for them.

SAIS

Raphael is armed with weapons called *sais*, which each consist of a long blade flanked by two short, sharp prongs. Raphael can use his *sais* to block an enemy's attack or to make a point of his own.

BEAT THIS!

"YOU DO NOT
WANT TO GO
UP AGAINST ME—
EVER!"

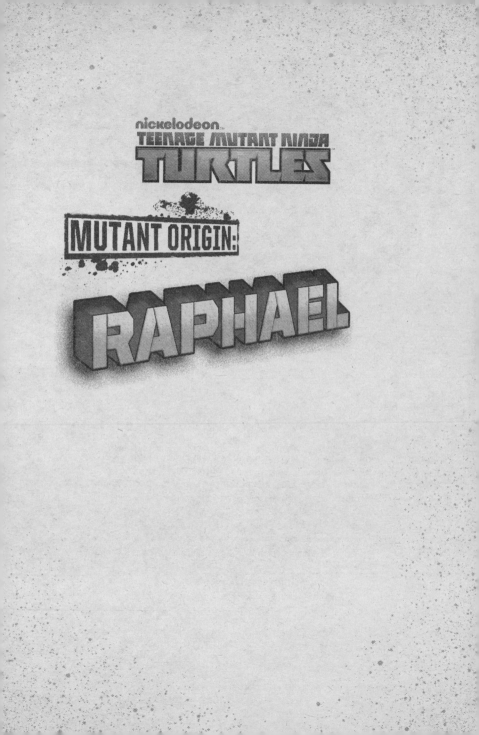

Published in the United States by Random House Children's Books,
a division of Random House, Inc., 1745 Broadway, New York, NY 10019,
and in Canada by Random House of Canada Limited, Toronto.
Random House and the colophon are registered trademarks of
Random House, Inc. Nickelodeon, Teenage Mutant Ninja Turtles,
and all related titles, logos, and characters are trademarks of
Viacom International Inc. and Viacom Overseas Holdings C.V.
Based on characters created by Peter Laird and Kevin Eastman.

ISBN: 978-0-449-80994-5

Printed in the United States of America
10 9

nickelodeon

TEENAGE MUTANT NINJA TURTLES

MUTANT ORIGIN:

RAPHAEL

Adapted by Michael Teitelbaum

Based on the teleplay "Day One, Part One"
by Joshua Sternin and Jeffrey Ventimilia

RANDOM HOUSE 🏠 NEW YORK

CHAPTER 1

My name's Raphael. What? You wanna make something of it? Okay, then. I'm glad we understand each other.

I'm a big green turtle like my brothers. We didn't start out this way, but Mikey already told you about how we went from little pets to the guys we are today.

Each of my brothers can do something special. Leo is pretty smart, except for the fact that he likes to watch that dumb TV show *Space Heroes*. I just don't get what's so exciting about watching a bunch of television characters pretending to be heroes. I wish he would loosen up a little, too. He's pretty stiff.

Donnie is real good with gadgets and computers and building stuff.

Me, I kick some serious butt in a fight. You do not want to go up against me—ever!

And Mikey, well, Mikey is real good at, at, uh—well, I'll have to get back to you on that one.

So as Mikey was telling you, Splinter, our kinda father, finally gave us the okay to leave our lair and go aboveground. If you ask me—which nobody did, by the way—

I'd say that Splinter treats us like we were still babies. I mean, we're fifteen, for crying out loud.

We climbed up through that manhole cover and out into the streets of the big city. After I saved Mikey from having that truck turn him into flat green street goo, we all regrouped on the sidewalk. Looking around, I had to say the city was pretty impressive—the lights, the cars, the people, the smell. Well, I could probably live without the smell, but you get my point.

"The city is just full of possibility!" Leo said, gawking at the buildings. "There could be adventure around this corner."

He took a few steps and pointed down the block. "Or this corner." He spun around and pointed in the other direction. "Or this one. Or this one. Maybe not that one."

What a dork.

Suddenly Donnie cried out. "Will you just look at this!" He waved the rest of us over.

What? What had he found—an evil ninja waiting to attack? Some bad guys who need their butts whupped? Not a chance.

We ran over and discovered him staring into the window of a computer store.

"Look at all the computers!" he gasped. His mouth opened wide and he pointed at a big computer setup in the window. "Is that the next-generation cadmium processor with quantum encryption?"

I realized that he clearly was not actually asking me the question. He was fishing for me to say, "I don't know, Donatello. Is it?" Not so fast!

"*Nooo!*" I said, as if he had just told me that he had grown wings and learned to fly.

"I can't believe it!" Donnie said.

"Me neither. I am *so* in shock!"

"It is! It is!" Donnie shrieked with delight. "It's the next-generation cadmium processor with quantum encryption!"

"Well, heck, I coulda told you *that*!"

"Guys! Guys! Guys! Check this out!" Mikey shouted, pointing up at a bright flashing sign.

"It's a hand made out of light!" Mikey cried. Sure enough, the glowing sign showed the outline of a big hand.

"Look! Now it's an eye made out of light! And now it's the hand again. Now the eye's back! Now the hand! Now the eye!"

"Come on, genius," I said, pulling him over to the rest of the group.

What Mikey lacks in brains he makes up for in enthusiasm. And he is *very* enthusiastic.

"Look! It's the eye again!"

Mikey and I joined Donnie and Leo in the middle of the street.

"So where to next, guys?" Donatello asked.

Before I could say a word, a bright light washed over us. It was smaller than the lights on that truck that had almost creamed Mikey, but it was still bright enough to blind us. Behind the light, a high-pitched whine filled the air, hurting my ears.

"Bring it on!" I shouted, reaching for my *sais*. Finally, a little action!

Brakes squealed and the lights turned to the side, revealing a motor scooter driven by a teenage boy. The scooter screeched to a stop, and I decided to have a little fun.

I lunged at the kid with my arms up and growled at him. *"Raaaaaaaaaahr!"*

"Ahhhhh! Monsters! Real-life monsters!" he shrieked like a little girl. He turned his scooter around and sped back the way he'd come.

"Hey!" I yelled after him. "Who are you calling a monster, huh? You're not exactly a poster boy for good looks yourself."

As the scooter zoomed away a big, flat rectangular box fell off the back and landed on the ground near our feet.

I slipped my *sais* back into their holsters.

"Now, *that* was fun!" I said, chuckling. "'Monsters,' huh. Come to think of it, I kinda like the sound of that."

Leo got a panicky look on his face, as if he'd suddenly remembered something important, like that *Space Heroes* was on.

"We're too exposed out here in the middle of the street," he said. He glanced up at the rooftops of the nearby buildings. "Come on."

We rushed off, heading for a tall building. I started to climb up the metal ladder on the side, but when I looked back down, I saw Mikey lagging behind the rest of us.

Now what was he doing?

Then I spotted the box—the flat white box that had fallen off the scooter—in Mikey's hands. Why would Mikey pick up a dirty box from the street? Why does that doofus do anything? I reached the roof and joined Leo and Donnie, who were already up there.

I paused for a second and took in the

view from the rooftop. So much was going on—way more than ever happened in our lair. It was like all the cool stuff we'd ever seen on TV come to life.

The air was damp and kinda stinky, but I liked the way it felt on my skin, the breeze and all. The level of noise made me realize just how quiet our lives had been before this. A constant buzz filled the air. Then every so often a loud burst of sound would erupt—a car honking or someone shouting.

And that moonlight . . . wow! It even made Leo look good—and that's not easy to do!

"Where's Michelangelo?" Leo asked.

"He's coming," I said. "He had to stop and pick up a dirty box from the street."

"A what?" asked Donnie.

"It's a piz-ah!" Mikey announced, scrambling over the metal ladder and onto the rooftop. "That's what it says here."

"What the heck's a piz-ah?" I asked, staring at the box.

"Should we open it?" Donatello asked, reaching out and touching the side of the box.

"Careful," Leonardo said, holding up his hand. "It could be dangerous."

"Oh, for crying out loud," I said. "You have got to be kidding me. Dangerous? *Dangerous?* Give me that." Sometimes Leo is just plain ridiculous. He wants to be a hero like Captain Ryan, but he's afraid of a cardboard box.

I reached over, grabbed the box from Mikey's hands, and opened it. Inside the box was a disc. It was red and white except for the edge, which was brown. The smell coming from the disc was absolutely heavenly, like nothing I'd ever smelled before— and I'd smelled a lot of stuff in my time.

"I think it's . . . it's food," Donatello said.

I wasn't so sure. "It's not like any food I ever saw," I said. "I don't see any algae or worms."

"I'll try it," Mikey said, snatching the box back from me.

He pulled at the side of the disc and a triangular piece came away in his hand. Then he very carefully took a bite.

Mikey's eyes opened wide. "Oh, ah, *mmmmm!*"

He shoved the rest of the triangle into his mouth. "Oh, my . . . oh . . ." His eyes rolled back into his head and he groaned with delight. Then he let out a huge belch.

And then he realized that the rest of us were staring at him. "Yuck," he said quickly. "You guys won't like it. I'll take the rest." But we're no fools.

"Think again, genius," I said as my brothers and I all grabbed pieces of the piz-ah.

I shoved a piece into my mouth. Oh, yeah, Mikey was right! It was incredible! "I never thought I'd taste anything better than worms and algae, but this is really amazing!"

"I love it up here!" Mikey shouted, licking the last bits of red stuff off his fingers.

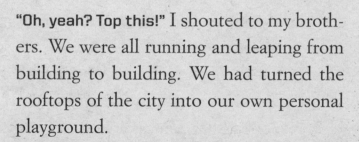

"Oh, yeah? Top this!" I shouted to my brothers. We were all running and leaping from building to building. We had turned the rooftops of the city into our own personal playground.

I took off at a breakneck pace, picking up speed as I ran along the rooftop. When I reached the edge, I went into a handstand and vaulted up into the air. I flipped through three somersaults. The alley between the buildings spun around again and again and again. Then I caught the edge of the next building with my toes, bounced high into the air, did a 360-degree turn, and stuck the landing.

"Now, *this* is fun!" I shouted. "We need to come out of our lair *every* night!"

"My turn," Mikey said. He ran, did a somersault, popped up and ran some more, did another somersault, then took a flying leap off the edge of the roof.

He sailed through the air, kicking his feet and whipping his arms around in circles. He looked like he was trying to swim through the sky standing straight up.

Mikey didn't quite make it onto the roof of the next building. He caught the edge with his fingertips and started sliding down the side. I was pretty sure he was going to crash into the garbage cans below, but he finally pulled himself up and rolled onto the roof, breathing heavily.

A vision of grace. That's my brother.

Donnie and Leo followed, and the four of us gathered at the far side of the roof, looking out at the lights of the city.

"I can't believe we've been missing all this for so long," Mikey said.

"You almost missed it just now, buddy," I said. I can never pass up a chance to bust Mikey's chops.

"I don't mean the roof, Raph," Mikey said. "I mean this whole big, beautiful city."

"Yeah, but we can't see the whole city in one night," said Leonardo, the world champion party pooper of all time. "It's getting late. We should probably head back home."

"Oh, man," Mikey whined.

"Paging Mr. Joy, Mr. Kill Joy," I muttered.

"Guys, wait," Donatello said suddenly, peering down to the street below. "Look at that!"

Donnie clapped both hands over his mouth. He had obviously seen something amazing. But what?

I leaned over the edge of the roof and saw a teenage girl walking on the street with a man who looked about the right age to be her father. The girl had bright red hair and a sweet smile. She wore a short-sleeved shirt and a pair of shorts. She walked down the street like she owned the city. It was her home. You could tell she had walked down that street hundreds of times before.

I still couldn't figure out what Donnie was so excited about. I mean, what was the big deal? They were humans. We'd all seen humans lots of times on TV.

"She's the most beautiful girl I've ever seen!" Donnie gushed, practically drooling on himself.

This was too good to pass up. "She's the most beautiful girl you've ever seen?" I asked. "Isn't she the *only* girl you've ever seen? TV doesn't count."

Donnie turned and scowled at me. "My point still stands," he grumbled.

"You mean the point at the top of your head, Donnie?" I said. Sometimes I just don't get my brothers.

"Joke all you want, Raph," Donnie said. "But I think I'm in love." Then he turned back and got moon-eyed all over again, dropping his chin into his hands to stare down at his one true love—a girl he'd seen from a roof for about twelve seconds.

"Yeah, sure." All this lovey-dovey stuff was gonna make me sick! Suddenly a big van came roaring down the street from out of nowhere and screeched to a halt right in front of the girl and the man. They both stopped short.

The side door to the van slid open and out jumped three big guys. Then the driver's door flew open and a small, skinny man jumped out.

"What do you want?" the girl's father said. Even from the rooftop, I could hear the panic in his voice.

"Leave us alone!" the girl shouted.

"We've got to save them!" Donatello shouted.

Yesss! Lovey-dovey time was over. Now it was time for some real-life, butt-kicking action—finally! I stepped up beside Donnie. Mikey joined us.

"Splinter's instructions were clear, guys," Leonardo said.

Leave it to Mr. Serious, Mr. Always-Follow-the-Rules, Mr. Splinter-Said, to ruin our shot at being real heroes.

"We're supposed to stay away from people," Leonardo continued. "And bathrooms."

Sometimes Leo just plain bugs me.

"I thought you wanted to be a hero!" I said to him. That girl and that man were obviously in trouble. "Since when do heroes ask for permission?"

"They don't," Leo replied. I could see he was trying to decide whether to do what Splinter said or do what he knew was right. "But—"

"Well, I'm going," Donnie said. Then he scrambled over the edge of the roof and climbed down the side of the building.

Okay. If Donnie was going, I wasn't about to sit on my hands!

I followed Donnie off the roof and down the metal ladder to the street below.

I landed on the sidewalk next to him, and Mikey was right behind. A few seconds later, Leo joined us.

All right! All four brothers working together for our first shot at being heroes!

We sprang into action. I grabbed my *sais* and charged straight at one of the three big guys who were trying to grab the girl and the man. But as I drew back my right hand, ready to puncture a few holes in the big dude's plans, I felt a sharp pain in my arm.

"Ow!" I yelled, spinning around, ready to do combat with another bad guy. Instead, I was face to face with Leo!

"Hey, watch it!" he yelled. "You bumped into my sword just as I was about to grab it and attack!"

"*You* watch it!" I shot back. Not the

cleverest comeback I've ever made, but,
hey, I was under a little bit of pressure. I
was trying to fight bad guys here!

I sidestepped Leo and squared off against one of the big guys. Timing my moves, I slipped my *sais* in again and again, landing blows on his arms and body.

Time to take this chump down! I stepped toward him, spun around, and grabbed his arm, getting ready to use my world-famous takedown throw.

Okay, maybe it wasn't world famous, seeing as the only parts of the world I'd ever seen were our lair and this street. But it is a really cool takedown move. I use my opponent's strength and weight against him. He ends up on his back with my *sais* at his throat. I find it delivers my message, which is: "I just kicked your butt!"

This time, things didn't work out as planned. The bad guy was really, really strong! I bent over to make my move, but I couldn't budge him—not one inch! It was like this dude was nailed to the ground.

That was when I felt a thick hand grab me around the waist, lift me into the air like I was one of those tiny turtles you get in a pet store—you know, like we all were before we took a bath in that green goo— and toss me aside.

Unfortunately, the big dude threw me right into Leo! I slammed into his shell and we both crashed to the ground. Again his sword whacked me.

"Hey!" I yelled, getting back up onto my feet. "You just jabbed me with your sword!"

"Well, I'm sorry," Leo snapped sarcastically, rolling over and leaping back up. "I didn't know you were going to land right where I was stabbing! What happened, anyway?"

"I tried to use my takedown throw on Gruesome here, but he wouldn't budge," I explained. "He just picked me up and flung me aside."

While Leo and I were sorting ourselves out and regrouping, Donnie was trying to rescue the girl. Or should I say his "one true love"?

The small, creepy-looking dude who had been driving was dragging the girl back to the van. What a total loser! I mean, I know I'm not Mr. Sensitive or anything, but dragging a girl through the street is just plain wrong. Always. End of story! This bozo was goin' down!

"Let go of me!" the girl yelled, struggling to break free.

"Yeah!" Donnie shouted. "Let go of her!"

Donnie's shout took the girl by surprise. She turned to see who had showed up to help her. She took one look at Donnie's big green face and let out a shriek.

"*Aiiiiiiiiii!*" she cried.

"Don't worry!" Donnie assured her, flashing a big smile. "It's okay. We're the good guys!"

"Oh," the girl replied. "Help me. They already took my father!" Then she looked Donnie up and down one more time.

"*Aiiiiiiiiii!*" she screamed again.

"No, no, don't be scared. I'm really nice once you get to know me," Donnie explained. "Just give me your hand!"

I figured he didn't have a chance, but

she reached her hand out to Donnie. He took hold of her and started to pull her away from the creepy little guy.

Donnie was looking like a real hero!

Unfortunately, that was when Mikey jumped into the battle and accidentally hit Donnie in the head with his *nunchucks,* knocking him away from the girl.

"Whoops. Sorry, bro," Mikey said sheepishly.

"'Sorry, bro'?" Donnie shouted. "That's all you got? 'Sorry, bro'? I had her, Mikey. I was a hero. I didn't need your help!"

"But we're supposed to be a team," Mikey said.

"And how did that work out, huh?" Donnie shot back.

"Go easy on him, Donnie," I said. I

don't like to see anyone pickin' on Mikey—
unless, of course, it's me!

While we were busy arguing, the creepy
little guy was busy pulling the girl into the
van. Two of the three big guys jumped in
after her, the door slammed shut,

and the van sped away, squealing and leaving skid marks on the street.

They left the third big bad guy stranded behind with us.

"Nice job, boys," I said, shaking my head. "I coulda done better by myself!"

Donnie just stared as the van drove away. At the same time, Mikey confronted the remaining bad dude.

"You think you're tough, huh?" Mikey blustered, up on his toes, shifting his weight from side to side as he spun his *nunchucks* in blinding circles. "You think you're tough enough to stand up to my hot *nunchuck* fury? Huh, punk?"

Mikey charged, slamming into the bad guy and whacking him with hit after hit from his *nunchucks*.

No reaction. The bad dude just stood

his ground as if nothing more than a fly had landed on him.

Mikey struck again, landing powerful *nunchuck* blows up and down the guy's body.

Still nothing. This guy withstood a pounding that would have brought a normal man to his knees. That made me wonder: If he's not a normal man, what is he?

Mikey tried one more time, but it was the same old story. The bad dude just took it like he was made out of stone.

"I see," Mikey said, slowly backing away. "Well, then . . ."

Mikey took off running. The bad dude chased him. I joined Leo and Donnie, and the three of us chased the van.

Now, this next part I'm gonna tell you about I heard from Mikey. I didn't see it myself, because I was off with my other brothers trying to save that girl and her father. And I know Mikey has a very active imagination. So I'm just warning you in advance. His story is pretty crazy.

Mikey dashed down the block and ran into a nearby alley. He turned to face the guy who had been chasing him. Thinking quickly, Mikey switched his *nunchucks* into their *kusarigama* mode, revealing the weapon's sharp blade.

"Stand back!" Mikey shouted.

But the big dude did just the opposite. He charged at Mikey and ran right into his blade. The sharp edge cut him clear across the midsection. And then—

Okay, here's the part I warned you about.

—and then the wannabe kidnapper started to spark and smoke. Yup, from the gash in his stomach! Red sparks and black smoke poured out of the gash.

"What the—?" Mikey couldn't believe his eyes. "A robot? This guy is a robot?"

The big guy stumbled in a haze, his eyes rolling back into his head. He lurched backward and fell to the ground.

"This is all kinds of wrong!" Mikey muttered.

He went over to the lifeless machine lying on the ground.

Suddenly a hatch on the robot's chest popped open and a thing that looked

like a brain with tentacles crawled out!
    It whipped its tentacles back and forth,
hissed, then leaped right at Mikey.

CHAPTER 3

Mikey told us the brain creature latched on to his face.

Naturally, Mikey screamed his lungs out.

Then he grabbed the thing with both hands, peeled it off his face, and threw it into a brick wall. The brain thing slid down to the ground. It hissed at Mikey, then crawled out of the alley.

That was when Mikey rejoined the rest of us.

We had chased the van for as long as we could before it sped out of view. We were trying to figure out our next move when Mikey ran up to us, out of breath and panicked.

"Guys! Guys!" he panted. "You're never gonna believe this! That big dude, the one that didn't make it back into the van, he—he—he had a brain!"

"We all have brains, Mikey," Leonardo said as patiently as he could.

"Not all of us," Donatello added, tilting his head toward Mikey.

"In our *chests*?" Mikey asked.

> Can I let you in on a secret? Mikey was right. But we didn't believe him . . . not then.

"No, Mikey, not in our chests," Leo added in that superior tone he likes to use. A tone I hate—even when it's not directed at me.

"You're not listening to me!" Mikey shouted, totally frustrated that no one was getting his point. Of course we weren't getting his point. His point sounded completely nuts. "That dude had a brain in his chest!"

WHAP!

Even I was shocked to see Leo slap Mikey. Then I remembered that episode of *Space Heroes* that Leo had been watching over and over again, and it all made sense.

Mikey shook his head, then stared at Leonardo in shock. "Did you just slap me?" he asked.

"I was calming you down," Leo said.

"What in the world makes you think that slapping me would calm me down!" Mikey shouted.

"I think Mikey's delusional," Donnie said to the rest of us.

Mikey looked as if his head were going to explode from frustration. "Just . . . just . . . come here!" he yelled.

He grabbed Leo's arm and started pulling him back toward the alley where he had battled the big dude. The rest of us shrugged, then followed.

"Guys, I'm telling you," Mikey babbled as he led us to the alley. "The big guy I fought was a robot."

A robot. Uh-huh . . .

"And he had a freaky-weird alien brain thing in his chest," Mikey continued. "You've gotta believe me, guys!"

"I'm not sure we do, Mikey," I said.

I mean . . . come on . . . a freaky-weird alien brain thing in his chest?

"Oh, yeah?" Mikey shot back. "Well, you'll change your tune when you see that he's . . ."

We stepped into the alley and Mikey pointed to the ground.

". . . gone?" Mikey said in shock. "He's gone? I'm telling you, his sparking, smoking robot body was right there on the ground."

Mikey shook his head and walked away, muttering to himself, "He was right there. . . ."

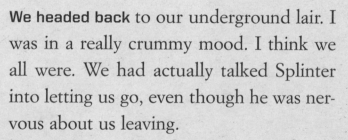

We headed back to our underground lair. I was in a really crummy mood. I think we all were. We had actually talked Splinter into letting us go, even though he was nervous about us leaving.

And what did we do? We went ahead and proved him right. We were not ready. We were not prepared. And so that girl and her father got kidnapped. And the bad guys got away. And Mikey almost got killed by some creepy alien stomach-brain-robot thing—that is, if you believe what he says.

We slipped into the manhole and climbed down the ladder to our lair. Splinter was waiting for us. No shock there. When we had gathered in the common area, we spilled our guts to Splinter. We told him everthing. Needless to say, he was really disappointed in us.

"Your inability to work together allowed them all to get away," he said.

"Well, maybe if I didn't have to waste time arguing with hero boy, *I* could have saved them," I said, glaring right at Leo.

"Hey!" he shouted at me. "If you hadn't gotten in my way, *I* could have saved them."

Then he turned toward Donnie. "And *you* went flying off on your own! How smart was that?"

Now it was Donnie's turn to get defensive. "It would have all worked out great if *somebody*—who shall remain *Mikey*!—hadn't hit me in the head with his *nunchucks*!"

Now it was getting just plain ugly.

"Oh, yeah?" Mikey shot back. "Well, *none* of this would have happened if *somebody* hadn't trusted us to go up there in the first place!"

Whoa!

Well, that shut us all up really fast. It took Mikey a couple of seconds, but then he heard himself, which for Mikey—who's kind of slow—was a pretty big step.

"Oh, jeez, Sensei," he said. "I didn't mean to—"

"No, Michelangelo," Splinter interrupted. "You are right."

"I am?" Mikey asked. He sounded surprised.

"He is?" I echoed. Using the words "Michelangelo" and "right" in the same sentence doesn't happen that often. I was shocked. And so were my brothers.

"You were not fully prepared for what was up there," Splinter explained. "I trained you to fight as individuals, not as a team. And as your teacher, your father, the responsibility for that is mine. Perhaps we can try again. In another year."

"Another year!" Donnie exclaimed. "Has everybody forgotten that people were kidnapped? They don't have a year.

Sensei, we have to do something now!"

Splinter shook his head. "I fear that allowing you to return to the surface would only be compounding my original mistake," he said.

"You weren't there, Sensei," Donnie shot back, practically shouting at Splinter. I'd never seen Donnie so angry. "You didn't see the way that girl looked into my eyes. She was scared. And she was counting on me—on us—to save her!"

I could see that Splinter was moved by Donnie's words. He glanced over at a photo of himself as a human with his baby daughter—a daughter he had lost. His eyes welled up with tears.

"Yes," Splinter said firmly. "You must save her."

All right! We were gonna get to kick

some more butt! I couldn't wait.

"I agree, Sensei," Leonardo said quickly. "But in that last fight we were not exactly a well-oiled machine."

"Like that robot with the brain-thingy," Mikey chimed in.

"Give it a rest, will ya, Mikey?" I muttered under my breath.

Splinter rubbed his chin and thought for a moment. "Hmm," he said softly. I could almost see his brain working. "If you are to fight more effectively as a unit, which you must do to defeat this enemy, then you are going to need a leader."

Leonardo's eyes lit up. "Can I be the leader?" he asked eagerly.

Big shock, right? Leo wanted to be the leader.

"Why should you be the leader?"

I asked. "I kicked your butt when we were sparring. I should be the leader." I wasn't about to let Leo get away with this.

"I'm smarter than all of you put together," Donnie said. "If we need a leader, it should be me."

"No way, it should be me!" Mikey cried.

Now, I love my brother Mikey, but leader material . . . I don't think so. We all stared at him for a few seconds, waiting to see what gem of a reason he was going to come up with.

"I don't really have a reason," Mikey admitted. "I just think it would be neat."

Splinter turned and walked from the common area. "This is a difficult decision," he said just before he stepped into his room. "I will meditate on it."

He went into his room and closed the door. About two seconds later he opened the door, stuck his head out, and said: "It's Leonardo." Then he closed the door again.

What? Why? Huh?

"No hard feelings, Raph?" Leo asked. That gloating voice made me want to punch him right in the nose.

"Stick it in your shell," I said, turning away.

Of course Splinter picked Leo, Mr. Serious.

CHAPTER 5

Late that night the four of us climbed up
through the manhole and back out into the
city. We searched until we found a building that had the same logo as the truck
that had carried off the girl and her father.
Climbing up to a roof that overlooked
the building, we hid in the shadows and
waited.

"Explain to me one more time what

we're doing here," Mikey said, pacing back and forth, itching for some action.

"Mikey, we've been over this," Leo began for the third time. "That building has the same logo as the van that the kidnappers drove. So if we wait here long enough, one of the kidnappers will eventually show his face. When he does, we'll make him tell us where they took the girl and her father."

Mikey nodded like crazy, as if he finally understood the plan.

"And then we've got ourselves a van!" he said.

No such luck.

"Just hit the guy I tell you to hit," Leo said, clearly not wanting to repeat the plan yet again.

"I can do that," Mikey said.

"Are you sure this is gonna work?" I asked. Part of me wanted to rescue those people and be a hero. But another part of me wanted to see Leo's plan fall right on its face.

"Trust me," Leo replied. "He'll be here any second."

Well, that was some new definition of "any second." We sat there for what felt like hours. Pacing, killing time, being incredibly bored.

After a while, Mikey and Donnie started playing a guessing game.

"Okay, I'm thinking of something green," Mikey said for the fourth time.

"Is it Raphael again?" Donnie asked, rolling his eyes.

"Man, you're good at this!" Mikey said, shaking his head.

I guess Mikey didn't quite get the point of the game.

Leo just kept staring down at the building with the logo. I have to give him credit. He is one determined Turtle. But that still didn't make him right.

"Give it up already," I said to him. "The guy's not going to show."

"We have to be patient," Leo said, not taking his eyes off the building.

"No, *you* have to come up with a better plan, Mr. Leader," I said. "Because the four of us standing here with our thumbs up our noses is pointless!"

Mikey stared down at his chubby green fingers. "I don't think they'd fit," he said.

"You sure about that, Raph?" Leo said, smiling.

I really need to work on my timing.

"He just showed up, didn't he?" I asked.

Leo's smile widened into a huge grin. That was all the answer I needed.

"I should have complained two hours ago," I muttered.

All four of us peered over the edge of the roof. There below was the slimy little guy who had shoved the girl into the van. Leo turned to face the rest of us.

"Gentlemen, I have a bold and daring plan," Leo said, doing his best Captain Ryan impression.

I wasn't about to stick around for the rest of that speech. I knew every word by heart.

Mikey, Donnie, and I climbed over the edge of the roof and crawled down the side of the building.

"There's no time for hesitation," Leo

blathered on, his voice growing fainter the farther away we got. "My orders must be carried out without ques—

"Hey, guys!" he shouted down to us from the roof once he realized we had all left. "Wait up!"

Mikey, Donnie, and I cornered the little creep.

"All right, buddy," I started, getting right up in his face. "We can do this the easy way or—my vote—the hard way."

Donnie stepped up beside me, crowding the guy. "Look at it logically," he said. "There's four of us and one of you. What can you do except tell us where you took the girl?"

In response, the little creep pulled out a freaky-looking weapon and fired an energy blast that knocked us all to the ground. Then he ran for the van.

"You had to ask, didn't you, Donnie?" I shouted as we all got back to our feet and ran after him. "You just had to ask what he could do."

The little guy jumped into the van, but I wasn't about to let him get away again. As it squealed off, I jumped onto the roof, hanging on for dear life.

The guy sped up and swerved from side to side, trying to shake me off. I dug in, grabbing the roof as tight as I could, but the momentum of the skidding van was too much.

I flew off the van and fell into the street. My brothers ran up to me.

"He's getting away again!" Donnie shouted.

Leo gritted his teeth. "No, he's not. Follow me!"

Leo led us back up to the roof. Running and leaping from rooftop to rooftop, cutting corners to gain on the van, we managed to catch up with him.

The little weasel looked up and saw us. He fired his energy weapon, forcing us to duck out of the way.

Leo pulled out a *shuriken,* a razor-sharp ninja throwing star. He aimed carefully and hurled the *shuriken* right at the van. It punctured one of the tires and the van went flipping end over end until it finally came to a stop.

"Now we're getting somewhere," Leo said.

We followed Leo down to the street. He and Donnie headed to the front of the overturned van. Leo gave me a hand signal. I had no idea what he was trying to tell me.

"Leo, I don't know what those funny hand movements mean!" I shouted.

"Raph, Mikey, go around to the back of the van!" Leo shouted.

"Why didn't he just say so?" Mikey whispered to me.

"It's Leo, our fearless leader," I replied, heading around to the back of the van with Mikey. "Don't try to figure him out."

"Ready?"

Mikey nodded.

I flung open the back door of the van. A canister exactly like the one Splinter had shown us before—the one that changed us all those years ago—tumbled out of the van, hit the ground, and rolled over to Mikey, stopping at his feet.

He looked down, wide-eyed.

"Mom?" he asked in a choked-up voice.

Near the front of the van, the little snaky guy was lying unconscious in the street.

We had captured him. We still needed to find that girl and her father, but we had learned a lot from our first adventure. For starters, we knew that we would have to work together as a team to succeed.

But more than that, we now knew where we came from. And we'd finally met the people behind the green goo that made us who we are. Now we just have to figure out exactly who they are and what they're up to.

And then we can kick their butts!